This book belongs to:

Catherine

Denton

HERRINGTON TEDDY BEARS

Presents

The Adventures of Harry & Hannah

COSTA MESA, CALIFORNIA U.S.A.

Printed and bound in China.

For information, contact:
Herrington Teddy Bears,
150 McCormick Avenue
Costa Mesa, California 92626 U.S.A.
(714)540-6657
www.herringtonteddybears.com

Library of Congress # 2002113303
ISBN: 0-9722343-0-6

Harry & Hannah:
The American Adventure

Written by

Chris Herrington

With Jean Ahern Lubin

Illustrated by

Jorge Pacheco

Once upon a time there were two little bears named Harry and Hannah Herrington. Not only were they brother and sister, they were twins! They both had fluffy honey-brown fur and big brown eyes, and of course, they had the same birthday! Every summer they got to visit their grandparents in the country for two whole weeks.

The first morning after breakfast, Grandma poured them each a tall glass of lemonade and then settled down to finish her mending. Before long, Harry and Hannah felt like doing some exploring.

"Why don't you go look through the old attic?" suggested Grandpa, peering at them over his glasses. The twins agreed that this was a great idea, and off they went, climbing up the creaky attic stairs.

Grandma and Grandpa's attic was full of boxes, trunks, old clothes and even a model of an old clipper ship that Grandpa had built when he was young.

"This looks just like a real ship!" Harry commented as he picked it up and blew off some dust. The dust sparkled in the sunlight.

"Wait!" cried Hannah, looking at the ship. "This piece of paper just fell out of it!" She picked up a roll of paper, tied with a red ribbon. "Let's open it and see what it says!"

They untied the ribbon and laid the paper flat on a table.

"Hey, it's a map. It looks very old. It's the United States!"
Hannah said, pointing.

Harry studied the map. He began to read aloud:

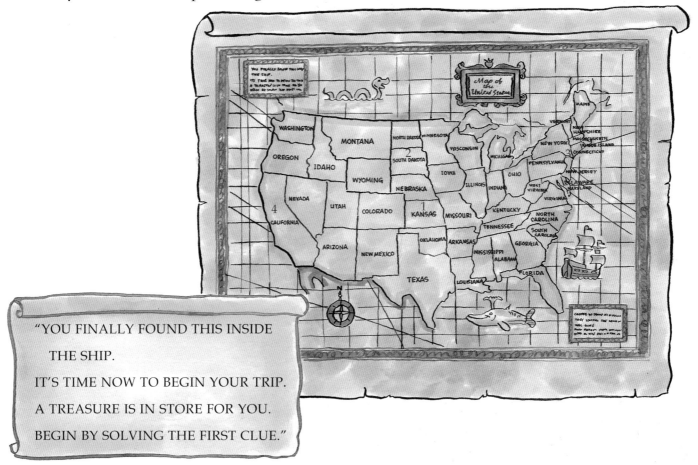

"YOU FINALLY FOUND THIS INSIDE
   THE SHIP.
IT'S TIME NOW TO BEGIN YOUR TRIP.
A TREASURE IS IN STORE FOR YOU.
BEGIN BY SOLVING THE FIRST CLUE."

"It looks like the number 1 is placed right where we are, at Grandma and Grandpa's house," observed Hannah. "Maybe the other numbers show us where to find the rest of the clues."

"I've always wanted to go on a treasure hunt! Let's go!" exclaimed Harry.

"Yes, but we'd better tell Grandma first," Hannah reminded him. The bears hurried downstairs to show Grandma what they had found.

Grandma looked over the map with a smile and suggested they pack a nice lunch before leaving on their adventure.

Hannah packed three plums and Harry put several corn muffins into their basket.

"Let's ask Grandpa what to do! He knows everything!" they decided.

Grandpa helped them read the first clue:

"CARVED IN STONE BY A FATHER AND SON, THEY STOPPED THE WORK BEFORE IT WAS DONE. FOUR FAMOUS MEN MADE THEIR QUOTA, DEEP IN THE HILLS OF SOUTH DAKOTA."

Harry and Hannah were puzzled. What could the clue mean?

"It looks like you're going to have to go to the hills of South Dakota to find out for yourselves," Grandpa explained. "But I will tell you that it has something to do with four presidents of the United States — Washington, Jefferson, Lincoln and Roosevelt."

"Mount Rushmore!" said Harry, pleased he had figured it out.

"But what about the first part of the clue?" Hannah wondered.

"Well," Grandpa told them, his eyes twinkling, "the sculptor was Gutzon Borglum — and his son worked with him! Also, the sculptor's original plan was to carve the presidents all the way down to their waists!"

GEORGE WASHINGTON

THOMAS JEFFERSON

ABRAHAM LINCOLN

THEODORE ROOSEVELT

Sure enough, number 2 on the map was smack dab in the state of South Dakota.

Grandpa chuckled knowingly. "You'll be gone and back in time for supper." He gave them each a kiss on the cheek.

"You see," said Grandpa whispering, "it's time for me to tell you a special secret. All the Herrington bears have an uncommon talent. If we think about a place very hard, and close our eyes very tightly, we can imagine ourselves anywhere we want to be. Just try it and see."

Harry and Hannah couldn't say a word, they were so excited. They held hands, and closed their eyes very tightly. They took a deep breath, and imagined Mount Rushmore with all their might.

When they opened their eyes, they couldn't believe what loomed before them!

"Awesome!" said both bears together. They gazed at the huge carved heads of the four presidents, rising 6,000 feet above them. They had to crane their necks to see it all. The majestic scene filled them with silent wonder.

Finally, Harry spoke up. "Well, now what?"

"Let's look for the second clue!" said Hannah.

The two bears started up the mountain across from Mount Rushmore. They climbed and climbed and climbed until they couldn't take another step. They decided to stop for lunch in a nice shady patch under a tree for a perfect view.

"Could I have the last muffin?" Hannah asked.

Just then they heard a funny squawking voice above their heads. "Excuse me."

Looking up, they saw a majestic eagle perched on a rock high above them.

The eagle, now that he knew he had their attention, continued. "How do you do? My name is True Blue Eagle and I haven't eaten in days. Do you think I could possibly have that last corn muffin?"

"You must be very hungry," said Hannah, feeling sorry for the beautiful eagle. She looked longingly at the last muffin. Harry nudged her, and Hannah held the muffin up for the eagle. "Here you go, True Blue."

The eagle swooped down and gobbled up every last crumb. "Thank you for sharing your lunch with me. I feel so much stronger! In fact, why don't you jump on my back?" He winked. "I know you're on a special mission!"

Before they could utter a word, True Blue scooped them up. The bears held on tight to the eagle's back as he soared up, up, up through the air and circled over the trees and right past the top of George Washington's head! What a ride!

"Thank you, True Blue Eagle!" they said.

The bird answered, "Thank you kindly for giving me food when I was so hungry. Now go find your next clue!" With that, the eagle flew out of sight.

Now a certain old buzzard had been watching the twin bears from a distance.

"Clue?" he muttered to himself, "Why, a clue can only mean one thing...they are on a treasure hunt!" Buster Buzzard decided then and there that he would find the treasure first by tricking the little bears!

"But first I must look my very best," he cackled with a sinister grin.

Buster Buzzard decided to put on his best maroon cap with a big fluffy feather in it, and his satin waistcoat with a real gold pocket watch.

Buster flew up to the little bears and gave a gracious bow. "How do you do? I am Buster Buzzard...at your service!"

"How do you do? I am Harry Herrington."

"I am his twin sister, Hannah Herrington." The bears bowed courteously. They were very impressed with this handsome-looking buzzard. They didn't realize he'd stolen everything he was wearing — including the watch — from tourists while they were visiting Mount Rushmore.

"May I be of assistance? Perhaps you'd like a guided tour of this famous monument?"

"Oh, thank you, I wish we had time," replied Hannah, "but that's not what brought us here."

"Yes," added Harry, looking around to make sure nobody was listening. "We're here to find a clue! Have you seen a little piece of rolled-up paper anywhere?"

"It should be tied up with a little ribbon," Hannah whispered to the shifty old buzzard.

"As a matter of fact," Buster replied, "I did see such a paper the other day...resting on the top of President Roosevelt's mustache!"

With a flurry of feathers, he was off! Buster grabbed the paper with his beak, and as he headed up toward the clouds he thought how nice it would be just to take the clue himself and never see the bears again. Then he would have the treasure all to himself! There was only one problem: Buster couldn't read! So instead he turned around and gave the clue to the eager little bears.

"Here you are, my furry friends!" Buster placed the roll of paper at their feet with a flourish. Harry and Hannah were very excited. They removed an elegant white ribbon, opened the paper, and began to read aloud:

"OFF TO A BUILDING YOU WILL GO,

SO HIGH IN THE CLOUDS, IT RAINS BELOW.

BUILT ON A NOISY ISLAND, TOO.

ITS STORIES ARE ONE HUNDRED AND TWO

"A building so tall you can stand on top and watch it rain below you? No such thing!" Buster announced with certainty.

"Well Buster, actually," Harry replied kindly, "I read a book once about New York City, and it *is* on an island — it's called Manhattan."

"Yes, that's right!" Hannah added, "and it's full of lots of traffic and lots of people — that's the noisy part!"

"And there is a building there that has 102 floors. It's the Empire State Building! When it was built, it was the tallest building in the world!"

Now that Buster had the information he wanted, he went back to being his usual, nasty self. "Give that to me!" he screeched, as he grabbed the clue and flew away. "Mine, all mine! The treasure will be all mine!" Buster snickered gleefully. As he rose higher, his best maroon cap with the big fluffy feather blew off, and the gold pocket watch fell from his grasp, but he held tightly to the scroll and pressed on towards the horizon.

Harry and Hannah watched as Buster disappeared to the west.

"Buster's flying the wrong way! He doesn't realize that New York City is east of here." said Harry.

Hannah nodded. "Buster will soon learn the hard way that being greedy won't get him anywhere. OK, Harry, let's go!"

The twin bears held hands, and squeezed their eyes shut.

When they opened their eyes, a magical skyline shimmered in the afternoon sunshine. Harry and Hannah had never seen such a bustling and vibrant city. So many tall buildings in one place — and the Empire State Building was certainly one of the tallest!

Soon they were standing on a busy street, looking straight up at the Empire State Building!

"I wonder where the third clue will be," mused Hannah. "Let's start at the top!"

"Good idea," answered Harry. They entered the building and hopped into the elevator. They'd never seen so many buttons in so many rows! 102 floors! They pushed the very last one, and with a whoosh the elevator started to rise. Their ears popped on the way up!

A few minutes later, they walked out on the observation deck on the 102nd floor of the Empire State Building. Everything looked so small down below!

"We're higher than the clouds!" shouted Harry, delighted. Hannah was already searching for the clue.

"Did you lose something?" A little pigeon stopped pecking at bread crumbs long enough to cock his head at Hannah.

"My brother and I are looking for a clue. It's written on a rolled-up piece of paper."

"Tied up with a ribbon?" The pigeon finished her sentence.

"You've seen it!" Hannah jumped up and down with excitement, as Harry rushed over to join them.

"Oh, I've seen it, all right..." The pigeon looked up to the highest part of the Empire State Building, the long pointed spire. There, swaying in the breeze, was the third clue — a rolled-up paper tied with a blue ribbon, neatly fastened to the very tip-top of the spire!

"Mr. Pigeon, do you think you could fly up and get the clue for us, before it blows away?" asked Harry.

"I would..." the pigeon said with his head down, "but I'm afraid of heights!"

"But how in the world did you get to the top of the Empire State Building?"

"Oh, that," he said, embarrassed. "I was born right up here. It was really fun — when my family was with me. But now I wish I could join them over in Central Park." He shifted his feet. "It's kind of lonely up here without them."

"What's your name?" Hannah asked sweetly, as she stroked his smooth feathers.

"I don't really have a name. The other birds just call me Scaredy Cat."

"Hey, you're no scaredy cat if you can live up here on top of one of the tallest buildings in the world!" said Harry. "I've seen millions of pigeons in parks, but very few up on top of the Empire State Building!"

Hannah nodded. "It takes a very special pigeon to live way up here above the clouds... a very brave pigeon. I'll bet you could do anything if you just tried!"

"In fact," said Harry, "a pigeon like you deserves a special name, a strong name." The bears thought for a moment.

"I know!" Harry brightened. "Let's call you Manny — Manny from Manhattan!"

The pigeon sniffed and smiled. "Manny?" He started strutting proudly, "Hey, I'm Manny! Manny, that's me!"

The bears clapped their hands. Harry patted Manny on the head and said, "You've got to believe you can fly! I know you can!"

By now the bears had forgotten all about the third clue. They were too busy encouraging their new friend. Suddenly, Manny began to flap his wings. He flapped faster and faster. Soon the little pigeon was up in the air, flying in circles!

"Hey! Watch me fly!" Manny did a somersault in the air followed by a back flip. Then he carefully plucked the ribboned paper from the spire of the Empire State Building and brought it back to the bears.

"Thank you, thank you!" the pigeon called. "You've given me something more precious than any treasure. I have confidence! Good-bye, little bears, I'll never forget you!"

Harry and Hannah waved as Manny headed toward Central Park to join his family.

"I'm sure glad we could help him," Harry said thoughtfully. Suddenly they remembered the clue. They opened the paper and read it together.

"THIS MIGHTY BRIDGE LINKS SHORE TO SHORE
WHILE STANDING ON THE OCEAN FLOOR
IN SEVEN YEARS THE WORK WAS DONE
SHINING GOLDEN IN THE WESTERN SUN."

"The Golden Gate Bridge!" the twins cried together. "On to clue number 4!"
They wished very hard with their eyes shut tight...

…and in an instant they were standing in the warm California sun.

"It's beautiful," Hannah sighed, gazing at the Golden Gate Bridge, "and it's so long!"

"Almost 2 miles long!" Harry added. "But let's get looking for the last clue!"

"Where could we possibly look?" whined Hannah, getting a bit tired.

"I don't have a clue," replied Harry, giggling at his own play on words.

They sat on the rocks, wondering what to do next.

"Ouch!" said a deep-toned voice. Harry jumped up.

"Who said that?" he asked.

"I did. I'm Trusty Tortoise," replied the giant turtle. "Don't worry, everybody thinks I'm a rock at first. What are you bears doing in my neck of the woods?"

"We're looking for a clue — a piece of paper tied with a ribbon. Somewhere around the Golden Gate Bridge," Hannah answered. "Have you seen any such thing?" asked Harry.

"Let me think," said the gentle tortoise. He thought and thought for such a long time, that Harry and Hannah got tired of waiting and fell fast asleep.

"I've got it!" Trusty Tortoise finally shouted. Harry and Hannah woke up abruptly. "There's an old fish who lives under the bridge. Monarch Fish, the King of all creatures around here. He'll know!"

The bears were excited. "Oh, please take us to him!"

Trusty Tortoise shook his head. "You could jump on my back if you want to, but it will take me at least two weeks to get down to the shore at my pace."

Because the bears knew they had to be home in time for supper, they thanked the kind-hearted tortoise and headed down to the shore on their own.

Suddenly, they saw a school of little fish in the water, darting back and forth. The bears asked if they could speak to the Monarch Fish, and all the little fish nodded in unison and scurried away.

A few minutes later, they returned, led by a very big, very grand, iridescent fish with purple-striped fins, wearing a golden crown with tiny jewels.

"Yes?" His scales shimmered in the late afternoon sun. The bears remembered their very best manners. "Oh Royal Highness, your most excellent Excellency.... We come from distant lands —"

The fish interrupted. "Forget all that fancy talk and get to the point." Relieved, the bears continued. "Have you seen a clue, a rolled-up paper?" asked Harry.

"Rolled up and tied with a little ribbon?" added Hannah. "You see, it is the last clue in our hunt for a hidden treasure!"

"Hidden treasure?" The Monarch Fish eyed them suspiciously. "Who believes in hidden treasure anymore?"

"*We* do," the bears answered, "because our Grandpa made a map for us, with clues!"

Just then a very tiny fish piped up, "I've seen a little scroll, rolled up just as you described, and tied with a ribbon! It's over there by the south pier!"

And off she swam. She returned a few minutes later, the final clue held tightly in her mouth, along with a little magnifying glass under her right fin.

"Thank you!" the bears squealed together. First they removed a silvery ribbon displaying 50 little white stars. As they unrolled the teeny-tiny scroll, a colorful broken fragment fell out. It looked like part of a medallion. Hannah carefully picked it up and put it in her pocket. Harry used the magnifying glass to read the final clue:

"THE AMERICAN PART OF YOUR HUNT IS THROUGH
A PIECE OF TREASURE YOU'VE NOW FOUND, TOO.
THE SECOND PIECE EXCITES LIKE THUNDER
SOMEWHERE AFAR IN THE LAND DOWN UNDER."

"The land down under," Harry exclaimed. "Hey, that's Australia!"

Hannah happily jumped up and down, pointing to the sun, which was starting to set in the west. "Let's go home now, and we'll get ready to go there tomorrow. We have to get back to Grandma and Grandpa's house in time for supper!"

The bears thanked their fish
friends, and waved good-bye.

They squeezed their eyes shut for the last time, and remembered how much they loved Grandma and Grandpa. In a blink they were back at their grandparents' house, sitting at the supper table.

"Right on time!" Grandma greeted them with a hug and a kiss, not the least bit surprised. "Did you cubs have fun today?"

"Oh yes!" Harry and Hannah started to tell Grandma and Grandpa all about their day, but Grandma told them to settle down, she couldn't understand them both talking at the same time.

Grandpa laughed as he took his place at the table. He filled his plate with a huge mound of mashed potatoes. "Your father used to love my treasure hunts too, when he was a cub."

Hannah held out her hand to show him the small piece of a medallion they had found. "Look, Grandpa...and tomorrow we're going to Australia to find the next piece of the treasure! I wonder what it will look like when we find all the pieces and put them together?"

"It will be something very special, I'm sure," said Grandma. "Now finish your supper, it's time for bed. You little bears have a busy day ahead of you tomorrow!"

That night, as they lay in their beds looking out the window at the stars, Harry whispered, "We sure saw some wonderful places today. It's an amazing country we live in."

Hannah sighed. "And I think we're about to discover that it's an amazing world too!"

The End

Welcome to the Wonderful World of Harry & Hannah Herrington!

Harry & Hannah are the central characters in a line of children's storybooks about two cute, cuddly little brown bear cubs that will forever be nine years old. Inquisitive and fun loving, the twins eagerly travel to new places and meet new friends. Travel along with them on all their globetrotting adventures!

Harry & Hannah are also the Herrington Teddy Bear Club's signature bears. Sign up for the Teddy Bear Club (see page 64) and join thousands of other bear collectors around the world who collect and trade Herrington Signature Collectibles.

The Harry & Hannah Collection

Herrington Teddy Bears has created an exquisite collection of handcrafted plush teddy bears and related characters inspired by the loveable twins' travel and adventures. It includes the bears and their friends in a variety of different sizes, outfits and options. From boxed sets perfect for gift giving to affordably priced key chains for parkas and backpacks, Harry & Hannah readers are sure to find something to treasure.

Major bookstores carry individual books as well as boxed sets, which include a book and miniature versions of the twins. Gift stores throughout the country sell 10", 14" and 18" bears dressed in outfits matching those worn in the books, as well as related clothing and accessories. You will also find the entire collection online at the Teddy Bear Club's website, **www.herringtonteddybears.com.**

The Adventures of Harry & Hannah

In Harry & Hannah: The American Adventure, the bear cubs explore the United States of America. While visiting historical landmarks, famous cities and the country's tallest buildings the bear cubs learn some important life lessons from animal friends they encounter along the way.

Companion sets feature the twins dressed in classic American kids style. Harry sports overalls and a red tee shit, while Hannah wears matching overalls and a rosebud print tee shirt. The Friends Assortment includes an 8" beanbag version of the five original characters introduced in the book: True Blue Eagle, Buster Buzzard, Manny Pigeon, Trusty Tortoise and Monarch Fish.

In **Harry & Hannah: The Christmas Adventure**. the twins travel to the North Pole, England and Switzerland before spending a magical Christmas Eve in New York City. Companion sets feature the twins dressed for these different events. For their holiday in New York, the twins are ready to go shopping on 5th Avenue or build a snowman in Central Park outfitted in leopard print holiday wear. Warm hooded jackets, color-matched knit scarves and white corduroy overalls are the perfect attire for their visit to the North Pole. A woven label on each bear's chest includes both the bear's name and the name of the adventure. A 10" Snowman Teddy Bear or Scout, the reindeer accompany either adventure set.

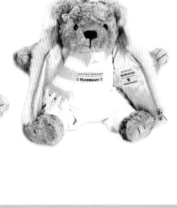

Harry & Hannah Special Edition sets are available featuring the bears dressed in outfits they will wear in upcoming adventures. See how the fuzzy explorers look as they tour Australia, Japan, Britain, South America, Africa and Europe in future storybooks.

HERRINGTON'S
TEDDY BEAR CLUB®

Herrington's Teddy Bear Club was created to provide a forum for collectors from all over the world to learn more about Herrington Teddy Bears. One of the most exciting aspects of collecting is learning about what has already been produced, as well as what is going to be released in the future. Members receive advance information about many upcoming collectibles designed by Herrington Teddy Bears for their impressive list of "signature brand" clientele.

For many years now, Herrington Teddy Bears has designed and produced collectible "signature" Teddy Bears for many well-known brands such as Hard Rock Café, Giorgio Beverly Hills, Mercedes-Benz, The Cheesecake Factory, Notre Dame University and many others. As a Member, you also have the opportunity to take advantage of limited edition Herrington Teddy Bears designed exclusively for the Club!

As a Member, you will also get advance news about all of Harry & Hannah's worldwide adventures, have the opportunity to pre-order new books, and have them personally autographed by company founder, Chris Herrington.

Club membership highlights include:

- Member's only collectible Herrington Teddy Bear
- Limited edition Member pin
- Member's only newsletter
- Member's only limited edition teddy bears
- Information on upcoming shows and events
- Priority notification of new limited edition teddy bear releases
- Access to Member's only area of website

And much more!

Harry & Hannah's Travel Passport & Medallion

Now that you own this book, you qualify for your very own Adventures of Harry & Hannah Passport. With the passport, you create your own storybook of the places you travel with Harry & Hannah on their worldwide adventures. Collect sections of the travel Medallion, like the one Hannah holds at the end of *The American Adventure*, to attach to your passport.

The passport and medallion sections are available only on our website, www.herringtonteddybears.com. You will need this secret code to apply for your free passport: "Lincoln". The medallion sections are ordered separately from the passport.

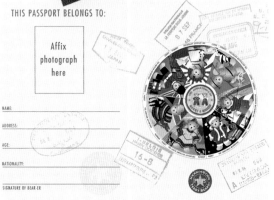

THIS PASSPORT BELONGS TO:

Affix
photograph
here

NAME:

ADDRESS:

AGE:

NATIONALITY:

SIGNATURE OF BEAR-ER

Credits & Acknowledgements

Book Design by:
Debra Valencia
devacommunications.com

Contributing Author:
Jean Ahern Lubin

Special Thanks to:
Ask Janis Editorial & Rewrite Services,
Editing and Proofreading

Northpoint Marketing Services, *Copywriting*

Martin Herrington, *Production*

Cecilia Gustavsson, *Production Assistance*

Russell Moore, *Photography*

Jorge Pacheco, *Illustration*

Jacki Ralph, *Public Relations*

Jonathan Sclater, *Illustration*

Sharilyn Sclater, *Illustration*

Miriam Bass, *Book Distribution*

All the staff at Herrington Teddy Bears

Finally, special thanks to the cute little bear cub that in 1902 captured the hearts of people all over the world and was the inspiration for the first "Teddy Bear."

Contact Us

Herrington Teddy Bears
150 McCormick Avenue
Costa Mesa, California 92626
Tel: (800)942-4498 or (714)540-7049
Fax: (714)540-0411
info@herringtonco.com

Distributed to the trade by
National Book Network, Inc.

Join Herrington's Teddy Bear Club or request your free certificate of authenticity for all Harry & Hannah Teddy Bears on our website.

www.herringtonteddybears.com